RESCUE

Illustrated by Tommy Stubbs

🅖 A GOLDEN BOOK • NEW YORK

Thomas the Tank Engine & Friends™

CREATED BY BRITT ALLCROFT

Based on The Railway Series by The Reverend W Awdry. © 2011 Gullane (Thomas) LLC.
Thomas the Tank Engine & Friends and Thomas & Friends are trademarks of Gullane (Thomas) Limited.
HIT and the HIT Entertainment logo are trademarks of HIT Entertainment Limited. All rights reserved.
Published in the United States by Golden Books, an imprint of Random House Children's Books,
a division of Random House, Inc., 1745 Broadway, New York, NY 10019, and in Canada by Random House of
Canada Limited, Toronto. Originally published by Golden Books in slightly different form in 2010.
Golden Books, A Golden Book, A Little Golden Book, and the G colophon
are registered trademarks of Random House, Inc.

www.randomhouse.com/kids   www.thomasandfriends.com

Educators and librarians, for a variety of teaching tools, visit us at www.randomhouse.com/teachers

ISBN: 978-0-375-87212-9

Printed in the United States of America

10 9 8 7

HiT entertainment

Thomas and Percy were helping to build a new Search and Rescue Center on the Island of Sodor. There was much work to do.

"It will be made of the strongest wood of all—jobi wood," said Sir Topham Hatt. "The wood will arrive today at Brendam Docks."

Diesel tried to move the logs by himself and had a terrible accident. Luckily, Thomas saved Diesel—but the logs fell into the sea.

Sir Topham Hatt was proud of Thomas. He asked Thomas to travel to the Mainland and bring back more jobi wood. Percy was worried that the trip would be dangerous.

A steamboat pulled Thomas on a raft toward the Mainland. Far out at sea, Thomas heard a loud crack.

"Fizzling fireboxes!" he peeped. "The chain to the steamboat has snapped!"

The next morning, Thomas found himself on a strange island. It was very misty. He peeped hello, but nobody answered. So he went exploring.

Suddenly, Thomas came fender to fender with three strange engines. Their names were Bash, Dash, and Ferdinand, and they called themselves the Logging Locos. Bash told Thomas he was on Misty Island.

Meanwhile, everyone on Sodor was looking for Thomas. Sir Topham Hatt and Captain raced out to sea.

Percy searched every track. Harold took to the sky.

Back on Misty Island, Bash, Dash, and
Ferdinand showed Thomas where they lived.
It was an old logging camp filled with winding
tracks and rickety cabins.

Thomas made an amazing discovery. "This camp is filled with jobi wood!" he peeped. "That's the wood we need to build the Search and Rescue Center!"

Thomas told the Logging Locos all about the Rescue Center. They agreed to help him collect the logs.

But the Logging Locos didn't like working. They just wanted to play games and bounce on Shake Shake Bridge. Thomas definitely did not like the wibbly, wobbly bridge.

Ol' Wheezy, the giant log loader, wasn't much help, either. He liked to throw logs, not stack them.

After much biffing and bashing, Thomas had flatbeds full of jobi logs, but he didn't know how to get back to Sodor.

Bash told him about an old tunnel that connected Misty Island to Sodor.

Pushing their flatbeds full of logs, the engines reached the old tunnel. It was cold and dark. The Logging Locos were scared.

"Don't worry," peeped Thomas. "With a whir and a whiff, we'll be on the Island of Sodor."

Suddenly, with a rumble and a crash, there was a cave-in! Rocks tumbled down around the engines. They were trapped—and no one knew where they were!

Thomas saw a hole in the roof of the tunnel.
He sent up puffs of steam.
Thomas hoped someone would
see the puffs and come to
the rescue.

Somebody did see the steam puffs—Percy!
"It's Thomas," Percy peeped excitedly. "He's
on Misty Island, and he needs help!"

Whiff told Percy about an old tunnel that led to Misty Island. Percy knew it would be dangerous, but it was the fastest way to save Thomas.

Percy raced through the tunnel. It was dark and twisty. At last he found the cave-in. "Watch out, Thomas!" Percy puffed. "I'm going to push back the rocks!"

Percy rocked and rolled and pumped his pistons.
CRASH!
Percy broke through the boulders. Thomas
and the Logging Locos were saved.

Sir Topham Hatt was very happy that Thomas and his new friends were safe. And with all the new jobi wood, the Rescue Center would be finished very soon.

"Today is a special day made possible by very special engines," Sir Topham Hatt said at the opening of the Search and Rescue Center. The people cheered. The engines all peeped. Thomas' pistons pumped with pride.